JACK
and the
Three Sillies

Told by Richard Chase
Pictures by Joshua Tolford

Houghton Mifflin Co., Boston
Riverside Press, Cambridge · Printed in
the U.S.A. · All rights reserved, includ-
ing the right to reproduce this
book or parts thereof in
any form.
Copyright 1950 by Richard Chase & Joshua Tolford

ISBN: 0-395-19100-9 REINFORCED EDITION   Ninth Printing   H

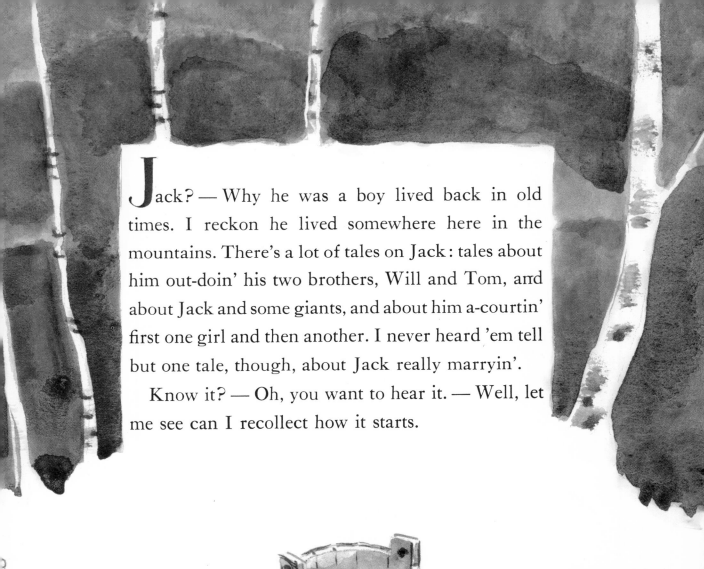

Jack? — Why he was a boy lived back in old times. I reckon he lived somewhere here in the mountains. There's a lot of tales on Jack: tales about him out-doin' his two brothers, Will and Tom, and about Jack and some giants, and about him a-courtin' first one girl and then another. I never heard 'em tell but one tale, though, about Jack really marryin'.

Know it? — Oh, you want to hear it. — Well, let me see can I recollect how it starts.

1

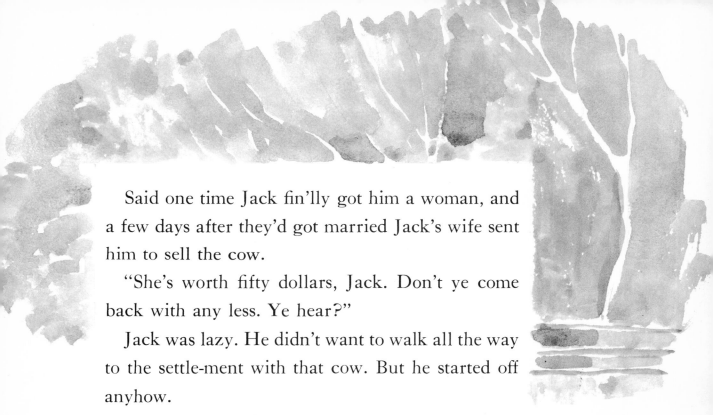

Said one time Jack fin'lly got him a woman, and a few days after they'd got married Jack's wife sent him to sell the cow.

"She's worth fifty dollars, Jack. Don't ye come back with any less. Ye hear?"

Jack was lazy. He didn't want to walk all the way to the settle-ment with that cow. But he started off anyhow.

Got along all right 'till directly his cow started actin' unruly. She went to balkin' and runnin' in and out the bushes, and Jack couldn't hold her.

4

Met a man drivin' a pig on a rope.

"Hello, Jack. You havin' a little trouble?"

"I never *saw* such a cow!"

The man helped Jack hold the cow.

"She's sort of puny, Jack. Looks old too. Now this sow is fat, and hit's a young one. How'd ye like to swap?"

Jack swapped for the pig, and went on.

But it wasn't long 'till that pig got unruly. Tangled Jack up in the rope. Old woman came along carryin' a goose.

"Havin' trouble, Jack?"

"Sort of," says Jack.

That pig had Jack so tangled and tied up he couldn't move.

"How'd you like to swap your pig for this goose, Jack? It'll not cause ye a bit of trouble. You can tote it under your arm — easy."

Jack swapped. Went on.

But directly the goose started actin' *awful* unruly:
went to floggin' Jack with its wings. Jack held on
to it the best he could.

Met a girl carryin' a big cat.

"Havin' some trouble, are ye, Jack?"

Jack had hold of his goose by one leg and was a-dodgin' and a-duckin', and it just a-whoppin' him and a-peckin' him.

"This goose — Ouch! — don't want — Ow! — to go — Dad burn this thing! — no further. — Ouch!"

The girl she helped Jack get the goose's wings folded down again 'till Jack could get a good grip on it.

"Why don't ye swap me for this cat, Jack? It won't be a bit of trouble to ye. Hit's a good 'un about catchin' rats and mice."

Jack swapped. Took the cat in his arms and went on.

But next thing he knowed, that cat saw a bird on a branch and tried to jump out of Jack's arms. Jack he held it tight, and it started scratchin'. So Jack squeezed it a little tighter, and that old cat went to meowlin' so loud and scratchin' Jack up so bad he was about to turn it loose.

Just about then a young feller came up, had a big round rock in his hands.

He set the rock down, took hold on Jack's cat and
got it tamed down again.

"A little more and you'd been a goner, Jack. Why don't ye swap me your cat for this round rock? It's an awful handy thing to prop the door back."

Jack figgered a rock wouldn't act unruly or peck him or scratch him, so he swapped.

Took that rock and went on back home.

"Where's my fifty dollars, Jack?"

"Fifty dollars? Huh! I never even got to town."

"Where's my cow, then?"

So Jack had to tell his wife how unruly her cow had acted, and how he had to keep on swappin' 'till he got that rock. —

"And hit's just fine to prop the door back. Here."

18

And he handed her that big rock.

She took it and threw it out in the yard.

"I'll say! 'Prop the door back'! I never saw such a silly in all my life. I'll bet there's no man in this whole world has got less sense than you."

"I'll bet there is," says Jack.

" 'Bet' — nothin'! I'm goin' to leave you this minute! That's what! And I'm not goin' to come back to ye neither, unless I find three men as silly as you are — and get my money back, too."

So Jack's wife she left him and started travellin'.
And one day she hadn't found a place to stay the
night, but the moon was full so she kept on travellin'
right on up in the night. She was walkin' past a
millpond, and there was a man over by the edge of
the pond a-jumpin' up and down and hollerin' and
a-throwin' his hands up and pointin' down in the
water. So Jack's wife went and asked him what was
the matter.

"It's the moon!" he hollered, and went to jumpin'
around some more. "Look! It's done dropped down
in the millpond! Right there! You can see it plain!

Law me! Run get some more folks to help get i
out! Get some ropes! Fetch a ladder! We'll hav
to get it out of there! O Law!

How'll we know when to plant 'taters and corn
unless we get the moon put back?

Get some ropes! Get a grabble-hook! Get a
ladder so we can put the moon back up in the sky
where it belongs!"

24

"That's not the moon. That's just where it's shinin'
in the water. Look up yonder. There's the moon.
Hit's in the sky."

" 'Look up'—nothin'! Why should I look up
yonder for it when I can see it right down there in
the water. Hunh! You must think I got no sense!
O Law! Somebody run here and help me get the
moon out!"

Jack's wife could hardly keep from laughin'.

"Don't just stand there!" that man told her. "I'll
hire ye to help! Here's ten dollars. Take it! — Take
26   it now, and run for help!"

And he went to hollerin' and jumpin' around
some more.

Jack's wife she put the ten dollars in her apron
pocket and went on. She told everybody she met,
and they all went up there to watch that man try to
get the moon out the millpond.

And after she got down the road a piece, she
stopped. "Well," she says, "that's one."

So she kept on travellin', and one day she saw an old man and an old woman in a field. The old man was hitched up to a plow and the old woman had hold of the plowlines. She'd flap the lines and whack 'em on the old man's back.

"Get-up there!" she'd holler, and the old man would heave on the plow.

Jack's wife looked and saw an old mule grazin' around in the field, so she stopped and watched. The old man would drag the plow a little ways and stop. Then the old woman 'uld holler and rattle the lines on him again, and he 'uld pull and heave the plow on a little further.

"Hey, you-all! Why don't ye hitch up that mule and plow with it?"

"Plow with a mule?" the old woman hollered back. "We *ride* the mule. We don't *never* plow with it. — Giddap!" And she whopped the old man again.

"Most folks do their plowin' with a mule."

"Ye say they do? — Well, anyhow, we don't know how to hitch up a mule to make it plow. — Get along there, old man!" — Kawhop!

"I can show ye how to hitch a mule to a plow."

The old man stopped, hollered out, "You show us that and I'll pay ye fifteen dollars, bedad!"

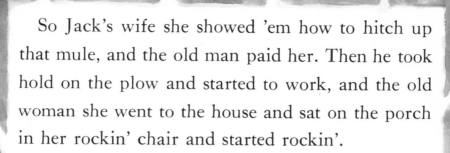

So Jack's wife she showed 'em how to hitch up that mule, and the old man paid her. Then he took hold on the plow and started to work, and the old woman she went to the house and sat on the porch in her rockin' chair and started rockin'.

Jack's wife went on.

"Humh!" she says, "That's two."

And she counted her money.

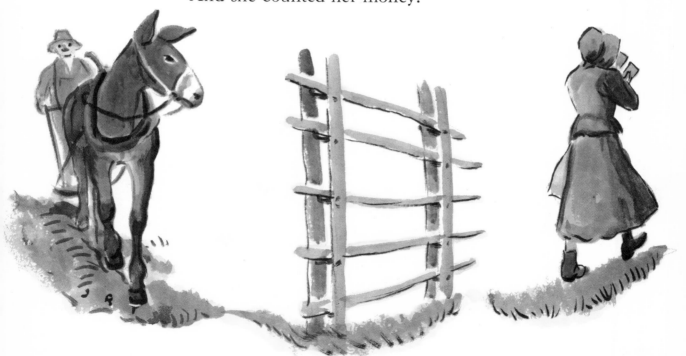

So she kept on travellin', kept on travellin', and one day she walked by a house that was close to the road, and all at once she heard somebody holler "Ow!" She looked and there sat a man on the porch, had a shirt on — sleeves and buttons and all — but his head was down under the cloth. His wife was standin' there before him with a stick of stovewood raised up. She bammed him on the head with it, and he hollered again.

"Hold still now, honey. It won't take but a few more licks."

— BAM! — "OW-W-W-W!"

Jack's wife stopped at the gate.

"What's the matter?" she asked 'em.

"Law me!" the woman told her. "I know everything about makin' a shirt except how to fix the neck-hole. I have to beat this old man's head through every time I make him a shirt. I don't make him one but once a year, and hit nearly kills him then. — Hold right still, honey. I'm goin' to have to hit it hard this time."

"Wait! I can show ye how to cut the neck-hole in a shirt."

That man he hollered out, "Show my wife that, and I'll pay ye twenty-five dollars, I will!"

So Jack's wife showed the woman how to cut and sew the neck-hole to a shirt, and her old man paid out the money.

Jack's wife went on.

"Well now," she says, "I reckon that makes three."

Then she stopped and counted her money — "A ten and three fives. That makes twenty-five. And two tens and a five. That's twenty-five more. And that makes fifty."

So she turned around and went on back to Jack.

And the last time I was down there they were both
of 'em gettin' on well.